Clint Faraday
book twenty
A Timely Burial

Bill Reynald's funeral is announced?

Well, that could piss me off! The least he could have done is tell me about it when I talking to him ten minutes ago!

Contents

About the author

CD Moulton has traveled extensively over much of the world both in the music business, where he was a rock guitarist, songwriter and arranger and in an import/export business. He has been everything from a bar owner to auto salvage (junkyard) manager, longshoreman to high steel worker, orchid grower to landscaper, tropical fish farmer to commercial fisherman. He started writing books in 1983 and has published more than 350 books as of January 1, 2023. His most popular books to date are about research with orchids, though much of his science fiction and fantasy work has proven popular. He wrote the CD Grimes, PI series, and the Det. Nick Storie series, Clint Faraday series, and many other works.

He now resides in Gualaca, Chiriqui, Panamá, where he writes books, plays music with friends, does research with orchids and medicinal plants. He has lately become involved in fighting for the rights of the indigenous people, who are among his closest friends, and in fighting the extreme corruption in the courts and police in Panamá.

He offers the free e-book, *Fading Paradise*, that explains what he has been through because of the corruption.

CD is the discoverer of the Chadam Protocol for curing cancer.

Facebook page Ambrosia peruviana for cancer.

A Timely Burial

<u>Interesting!</u>

Clint Faraday, retired PI from Florida now living in Panamá, was returning from Almirante to Isla Colón, where he had his home (one of them). He saw a man who lived on Isla Popa who he knew for more than four years on the deck at El Ultimo Refugio. He went to the deck and chatted about the situation on Popa and how the wife and baby were doing. Bill Reynalds had married a more than beautiful local part India/part Spanish girl a year and a half ago. She was the cousin of Clint's own beautiful wife, Tyna, who had returned to Bocas Town, Isla Colón, with Clint and their own six month old son, Clintonito (Nito) from a small town in the comarca, Quebrada Tula, just three days ago. They were going to raise their son mostly on the comarca in the Indio traditions. Clint had the great honor of being the second person ever to be declared Ngobe.

"I think this is paradise, Clint! I've died and gone to the heaven I don't believe in! The baby's three months old and I've only heard it crying two or three times. I was scared shitless about that, but Leyda laughs and said a baby cries for specific needs.Tthis baby doesn't need those things and is content. The only time it cries is when there's a damned good reason!"

"She's India, raised India," Clint replied. "The baby's always in contact with a parent, so it's secure. It doesn't cry to get attention. It already has attention."

"I very seldom ever heard an Indio kid cry," he agreed. "Even when they're three and four years old they don't go wild and try to be the center of attention. I heard a little kid, not more than three, ask his mother why two kids were acting so bad in the big China and she said they were unhappy because they weren't indigenos.

"I'm getting so I can speak Ngobe pretty well, now. I think she was right!"

"That's about what it comes to.

"Did you ever get that theft problem resolved?"

"Not really. I think that was nothing to do with the indigenos. Leyda says it wasn't. I can believe she would know or find out pretty fast. It wasn't that much, it was just the reality that it could happen to me. I'm willing to just write it off to experience. It taught me to take pre-cautions about certain things.

"I'm getting used to the people there coming into

the house and taking whatever they want. Leyda does that with them. If you need it, just say so. They won't think anything of it."

"You're learning that they don't have ownership, like everyone else. Another great thing about their culture. They aren't stealing, they're just using what's community property. You don't have it to the extent they do in the comarcas, but it will still be there in families."

"Yeah. I'm getting so I understand it and can relate. I needed a chain saw when mine quit on me and Quint wasn't home. I just took it and used it, then took it back. He was sitting there. All he said was he hoped I'd remembered to keep the oil full, because it leaked a little.

"I did. He was a little surprised that I'd filled the gas tank."

"That's the way it should be."

"I hope it doesn't change, but it will off the comarcas – and they're learning a bit of greed there now, what with the materialistic tourists.

"Damn! Whoa! Did you hear what I just said? *Me*? 'Materialistic tourists?' Christ! I was among the worst when I came here!"

"Welcome to paradise!"

They chatted for a few more minutes, then Clint went on home and carried the things he'd bought in David into the house. He was back out on his deck when Judi Lum, his attractive Oriental next door neighbor and a very big help in the detective business called that she just heard an announcement on the TV than might interest him. He knew a lot of those people.

"People?"

"The expats living on the islands and so forth."

"Oh. What happened now?"

"They announced that Bill Reynalds' interment is set for Saturday at ten. I know you knew him and his wife. I suppose you'll want to go."

"That *is* interesting! *Really* interesting!"

"It is? Why?"

"Because I was talking to him at Refugios not ten minutes ago. You would think he'd mention something like that!"

She laughed, and gave him the finger.

"Oh! Tyna will be back in about an hour. She's visiting family on San Cristóbal."

"Thanks, Jude. I'll call Bill and tell him I'm miffed that he didn't invite me to his funeral."

"Do you know any other Bill Reynalds?"

"No. I think there'll be an explanation. Somebody read the wrong name on something or other. Probably a Maria Smith is to be buried. That would be par for the course."

"Sadly, too true! Caio!"

She went back inside. Clint shook his head and

went inside to the house phone to call Reynalds.

"Yo, Clint! Problem?"

"I just wanted to know why you didn't invite me to your funeral. I had to wait to hear about it from the TV!"

"No kidding? I'm really dead? It wasn't just an expression?" he replied, with a laugh.

"According to TV. Judi saw it. I figured you'd want to straighten it out."

"Yeah, I guess I'd better. Thanks, Clint."

They hung up. Clint sighed and took a large lobster from the freezer. He'd cook up a gourmet dinner for him and his wife.

There was a "Buenos!" call from outside. Clint called "Passe!" and Ben and Earl, neighbors, came in.

"Clint, I just heard about Bill Reynalds. It was sort of a shock," Ben said.

"To him, too!" Clint replied. "I just told him about it."

"Oh. One of the normal fuck-ups by the media? Read the baseball scores on the obits?"

"I suppose."

"I have to know what you know. I'm on my way to Popa to talk with Bill," Clint said to Sergio Sanchez, chief of violent crimes with the Policía Nacionál.

"Very little. We're still trying to find how this happened. We wouldn't have even heard about it except for the TV thing. The ME in Changuinola said there was a slip of paper in his wallet that only said 'Faraday. Bocas. cpq.' That's you, but we haven't an idea what it means."

"How did John Doe die?"

"I'm having that looked into. Death certificate says natural causes."

"It could be, but I sort of doubt it. How was he identified?"

"Passport."

"He was a gringo, then?"

"So far as we know. There are a lot of gringos with Spanish and black features. It's getting hard to tell unless they're blond. Even that doesn't always mean much anymore. Lots of Suiza here now. Born here."

"He was black?"

"Mixed."

"Bill is a pale-skinned, light brown-haired man. He *looks* like a gringo."

"And this guy had a passport in his name and with the guy's picture. How did he get it?"

"Wild Bill had a collection of stolen passports. Reynalds was robbed a few months ago. One and one equals twelve point seven."

"Ain't that the truth!"

"Can you get anything from prints?"

"It's in process. We have DNA, too. It's getting more and more common to be able to find people through DNA trace."

"If he was a gringo, it shouldn't be hard to find who he was. The prints will come up from his real passport."

They chatted about various things. Clint went to the Golden Grill, where Judi was talking with the regulars. Jim and George were there, along with German Freddy and Kansas Tom. Tom, from somewhere in New England, saw him come in and suddenly had to go. He and Clint didn't get along, at all. There had been confrontations where Tom always came out third in a two horse race..

Clint greeted everybody and Judi said they were just talking about Reynalds. Nobody had a clue as to who the dead man might have been.

"What?!" Clint exclaimed. "Are you telling me Tom didn't know enough to tell you all about it?!"

Judi gave him the bird. Jim said that Tom, as always, had a theory. "He thinks the guy's someone he heard about in Changuinola when that mafia boss, Robinson, was asking about someone who was on the run from them. Robinson asked him about it because he knows everyone on Isla Colón and would know if someone was acting strange."

"Mafia? Robinson? Now Robinson's mafia, not just a local crook?" Clint asked.

"Well now, Clint! After all, Tom does know about that kind of thing, you know," Judi said, condescendingly. Jim and George laughed. Fred said he'd like to smack the damned obsequious swinehund in the chops, sometimes. He agreed with Clint about him.

"We don't have a clue. He's not from around here. I don't think I've ever seen him on the island," Jim said. "Probably just some guy who died naturally out in the jungle or whatever.

"What does Bill say?"

"I asked him why he didn't at least tell his close friends about his funeral. He doesn't have a clue, except that his passport was stolen when his place was burglarized a few months ago," Clint replied. "That's the thing that tells me it wasn't a natural death. I imagine we'll learn what it's about when we identify him. I'm going to talk to the mortuary in Changuinola this morning. I think I can learn something there."

"You can? How?" Fred asked.

"There were funeral arrangements? Who made them?" Clint asked.

"I'll be damned! Obvious!" Jim said. "Hell! I would have thought of that in a week or so, myself!"

They talked about a number of other things, then Clint went home to get his boat and head for Almirante. He kept his car there and would drive to Changuinola. He first went to the police station to find what they knew. There was a backlog in the labs in Panamá City, but they should have an answer in an hour or so.

This was Panamá. "An hour or so" probably meant sometime tomorrow afternoon. Or maybe the next day.

He went home to play with Nito for a few minutes and tease Tyna, then got his boat to head for the bay.

A couple of days in his home, then a case.

Well, it gave him something to do. He did like a puzzle.

"I'll look it ... I wonder why I never thought of that? It was such as shock to learn that the man we were about to bury wasn't the man it was supposed to be," Sra. Verona said. She ran the funeral home where the body was sent. She spent a few minutes reading the contract, then said, "How odd! He made the arrangements ... himself. Two weeks ago.... Prepaid contract.

"I'd say it was a timely contract, all things considered. It would take the burden ... but it wasn't him!"

"What identification?" Clint asked.

"It was ... here. Passport number. Notarized."

Clint read it over, thanked her, then went to the mortuary to talk to the ME.

"He died of what appears to be a deteriorated heart condition. He was found by the road near Cauchero. There was evidence of no one nor anything in the area, other than himself. He had stopped at the tienda for a juice and said he was going to walk to the break to get some pictures of the sea from the mountain, there. Gwendolyn, the woman who runs the store, said he was sweating, but it was hot. She didn't think much of it, except his color was wrong. He was a gringo, so she may have been wrong about it.

"Autopsy showed deteriorated muscle tissue. He over-exerted. It would not have become fatal, had he rested. He felt the pain, panicked, and died. Classical. The false passport may lead to other things, but he died of massive coronary."

Clint nodded. He soon left to go back to Bocas Town.

This guy might have died from a massive heart attack, but what panicked him, the thing that actually killed him, was probably someone, not a reaction to severe unexpected chest pain. He was walking along the road, slightly upward at that point. He was out of breath, sweating and tired. He had that condition for some time, so would know all he had to do was sit in the shade for a few minutes and it would subside.

Something or somebody had come along up there to literally scare him to death. Possibly it was someone who was following him, looking for just such an opportunity.

Clint went back to Bocas Town and to the police station. Sergio said they had an ID on the corpse. Henry Joseph Knotts. He was a zonie with a North American father and a Colombian mother, born in the zone, thus a Panamanian.

He was identified through DNA just before the prints, which confirmed. Both were on his pistol permits. He had three.

Pistol permits were granted if you could show good reason to have them. Sergio was bringing up his record on the computer.

"No criminal record. A few petty things. Loud

arguments with ex-wife. Fight with her brother. Challenge for custody of son, two years ago. Son was four years old. Hmm.

"Divorce for infidelity. Wife. Refused DNA test of son, but half-match to him was perfect. It is his son. Grounds for custody was that he divorced her for infidelity and she refused DNA test, thus she was afraid it wasn't his. Judge refused him custody. He claimed corruption and that she paid the judge off. No investigation ... that sorta shows it *was* corruption. They would investigate that one if the presiding internal affairs judge hadn't stopped it.

"The guy had a lot of legitimate gripes, you ask me!

"Personality profile suggests he became bitter. He got the pistol permits because the brother had threatened his life before witnesses. She had threatened to have some people she knew kill him if he didn't stop bothering her about the child. She had a restraining order against him and he had one against the brother.

"This is one sordid mess! He was shunned by neighbors because he was always so negative.

"There are little notes on some of the reports suggesting he had pretty solid grounds for his complaints, but no action was ever taken.

"Hmm. Here's an interesting little note on the

side of a complaint. Officer Zenares. 'Espa. prmo plia dsptch' with a question mark. Wife's cousin is the police dispatcher. This is in Chitre.

"So! What was he doing here?"

"Does it have an address in Chitre for him?" Clint asked.

"Hmm. Yes. He owned a house. About the only thing she didn't get in the divorce. Another odd thing. He got the divorce because he proved his case. It's not easy to get a divorce in Panamá. With this record, he should have gotten everything, including the child.

"Clint, this smells. What's going on?"

"Whatever, it damned well shouldn't be going on!

"Sergio, can you have that house sealed so no one gets in and appoint me investigative expert?"

"Done! I'll have Santos, in Panamá City, issue an order. If it comes from him and is violated, somebody will spend a minimum of four years in carcel."

"I'm on my way!"

"The chopper will take you. There will be a car waiting at your disposal. We can maybe scare a few of them, ourselves!"

Clint got out of the police chopper at Chitre and had the waiting car take him to the house. An Officer José Perez would be along to observe. Perez had made it very damned plain that he considered Clint an intruder into what should be a local police affair on the ride to the house.

Clint simply ignored him, from that point. He was met at the house by an officer from Panamá City, Irena Jaurez. She said she had orders to work with him, not with the local police. As a declared investigator, his orders took precedence. When she got him aside while Perez parked the car she said she was with the corruption board. There seemed to be a problem in the area. He understood she didn't want that fact known.

She said they had no keys. Clint had the set Sergio had from the body, so he was able to go in quickly. He went through and to the back to open the steel door there. Someone had gone to a lot of trouble to try to break in, but had failed. They had cut the padlock off of the outer steel gate, but the door was thick steel with a deadlock welded in. He noted that for the officers and returned to the interior. Perez had wanted to stay in the salon while Clint and the other officer checked the back of the house. Juarez said they were to be together at all times. There must be no question about what any of them did.

"What questionable actions could there be?" Perez demanded.

"I was only instructed to observe and to see that we were all together at all times. I think there was a questionable order from a judge or someone before where this man, Knotts, was concerned."

Perez was suddenly suspicious and nervous. Clint pretended not to notice as he quickly went from room to room. They returned to the salon where he said there was no evidence that anything was disturbed into the recorder he was carrying. He made comments as they entered each room. It was video-audio, so he had a good record. He saw the first place he wanted to search when they went into the master bedroom. He sat to give a concise rundown of what he'd observed. He said the house didn't seem to hold any clues as to what was behind whatever it was. He would spend some time looking for something, but the way things seemed from the first would indicate any important messages would be in plain view upon entering the house. None were in evidence. This may be a natural death that simply appeared to be contrived. The ME had explained that Knotts had muscle deterioration of the heart and was under undue physical stress. He might have panicked, as suggested, and died of a coronary. He would do a more complete check, but could almost guarantee there was nothing to find in that house. He managed to make it sound like he was totally disinterested and would prefer to be elsewhere.

He said they could go ... but he was there, anyhow, so might as well do a fast exam of the place.

Perez looked relieved and said he would stay if Clint wanted, but he had other duties a lot more important than looking through the leavings of some guy who had died of heart failure while climbing a mountain. Irena gave a slightly raised eyebrow toward Clint, but didn't say anything. She asked Clint if she should stay or whether his report was as much as done. He said she could stay or go. It was all the same to him.

Perez stepped outside and she moved quickly to just inside the door. She indicated he was using a cell phone. Clint grinned. She raised the eyebrow. Clint pointed to his shoulder where Perez had carried a radio. He had noted that Perez kept moving it around a bit as they changed positions while going through the house.

"Not police? Cellular?" she mouthed, silently.

Clint nodded.

She pointed to her ears and shook her head. She couldn't hear him. He was moving toward the police car. She stepped out to call that she would carry Clint back to the station. Probably ten or fifteen minutes.

She turned to ask Clint what the look was about when Perez said that about the heart.

"Nobody except the police medical examiner here knew when or how he died, only that he was dead. Perez knew heart attack in the mountains. Interesting."

They went back inside where Clint immediately went to the bedroom and the computer sitting there as soon as they saw Perez drive off. He turned it on and brought up the history in DOS. There were several entries lately to a file RSTRCT.cd.

There was a file that you had to bring up by typing in a code. It would not show on normal search. There was another code to open it.

He thought and put it back onto Windows. He typed in the file: Faraday. A code box came up. He thought a moment and typed: Bocas. The file came onscreen.

"How did you know?" Irena asked.

"He had a slip of paper in his pocket. It said 'Faraday. Bocas. cmq.' I didn't know what it meant unless he was going to see me about the treatment he was getting and the threats from his ex-wife and her brother. What the 'cmq' meant was open. This is a Compaq computer. It sort of clicked when I saw it sitting here.

"Let's see what he left for me. He expected to be killed, it would appear."

It was a list of dates and times and names. His ex-wife and her brother and a number of others.

"Okay. Here's Perez twice. Perez-Flako the fifth at nine o'clock. Perez and Dorcas sixth at nine o'clock.

"Here's a name I remember from the report Sergio read. Zenares. Zenares and Dorcas.

"Is Zenares still with the police here?"

She read a list. "No. He was transferred to Penonomé on the twelfth. Dorcas is dispatcher."

"So. She's the ex-wife's cousin. Who's Flako? Flako who?"

"Probably Fernando Flako. Officer on the patrol force."

Andres and Flako. Andres and Dorcas. Andres and Melendez. Who's Andres et al?"

"Don't know. Maybe the wife's brother or ... here it is. Andres Vanderas, is the brother of Filomena Sardina, ex-wife of Henry Joseph Knotts."

"Filomena? She met with all of them. When we

know who Melendez is we should have quite a little corruption gang!"

"Melendez is the judge I'm investigating. See if the dates they met, particularly Filomena and Andres, are in March. Before the seventh."

"Before and on."

"Bingo! We have their crooked asses, for sure! This should be enough in itself. Dead person's declaration!"

"We can hold it until we catch the one or ones responsible for his murder, okay?"

"Oh, yeah! They aren't going anywhere, for sure!"

They spent another few minutes checking the computer carefully. There was another secret file, but they didn't stand a chance of knowing how to open it. Clint wondered why it didn't come up on the DOS record.

He was making one final check when he noticed that there was a file in the virus vault. That was unexpected. Knotts had kept the vault emptied.

He went to the virus vault. It listed the file as *RVNG.exe: Trojan x-othr*.

A Trojan opened on a specific date or when a specific file was opened.

He was sure he knew how to open it. He had an idea it wouldn't be a good idea to open that file yet. He would need some protection for the computer. It might be one of those things that destroy the hard drive.

There was a question mark in the source file box. The date was just last week. It was all too possible someone had suspected the secret file on the computer and had put the virus in, thinking anyone who came across it would ... that anyone opening the secret Faraday/Bocas file would automatically release the virus. The file would become meaningless in two seconds. The hard drive would be erased.

Clint didn't think so, but it could wait.

"We have what we need here, and then some. What next?" Irena asked.

"I want to talk with his doctor. I want to know something about the timing."

"The timing?"

"I have a few questions about this. Maybe the doctor can answer some of them.

<u>*Doctor, Doctor, Gimme the News*</u>

"Doctor Rodriquez? I'm Clint Faraday. We're investigating the death of one of your patients, Henry Knotts. Could you give me a rundown on his health problems?"

"Henry? Yes. Sad thing. His heart was in poor condition, but I never thought it was critical. I was concentrating on the other things.

"I don't have much information. The police wanted to know only if he had a bad heart. If so, it would explain his death."

"He was in the mountains, had walked about two kilometers uphill at a low angle, was short of breath and pale, according to the woman who sold him a juice at a stand. He was found laying by the road. The ME said he died of heart failure, but that it was the kind of thing where he would know that all he had to do was sit still for a few minutes and it would subside. He theorized that he panicked and died more from fright than the actual heart condition."

"He didn't think the cancer was a contributing factor?"

"Cancer? He didn't mention cancer!"

"Henry had a small cancer of the brain that was arrested, but inoperable. It would activate at some indeterminate time and kill him. He knew it and was fatalistic about it. We have several therapies we were using to keep it in remission, but we both were aware that his time was very limited. It was why I didn't worry so very much about the deteriorated heart muscle. He would more than probably die from the cancer than from the heart problem."

"Would he know if it was activating?"

"Yes. He had some dull undefinable pain when it was growing from the internal pressure. We had managed to relieve it, twice. He would know if it was returning.

"I see. Was he suicidal at such times?

"No, though he would ... he might have known some pressure and would want to go to some final place or see some last sunset or something. He would not fight the heart problem because it would be faster and cleaner than the cancer death.

"Yes, Mr. Faraday. That's quite possible. He wouldn't commit suicide, but he wouldn't slow the time of death in such a case. If he were there because he wanted to die in that place with that view or something, he might well have decided not to fight the heart attack. He might have deliberately overstressed his heart, knowing it would prove fatal very quickly. He was used to pain, so the intensity of the final attack would not be something he couldn't endure.

"He has had a very unpleasant life for the past four or five years. While he might not end it, himself, he would also not fight death."

"I see. I figured something like that, but there was a question of whether some people did something to, shall we say, hasten his death."

"Andres? He's thoroughly capable. He and his sister are despicable people. If that were at all possible, I wouldn't blink!

"Mr. Faraday, it shouldn't be too difficult to learn if Andres – or even Filomena – were not here when he died. It would be most telling if one or even both of them were shopping in David or something, wouldn't it?

"Mr. Faraday, does the medical examiner still have the body? I have thought of something."

"I think so."

"Please call and have him check Henry's body for such things as digitalin."

Clint registered surprise. Rodriguez pointed to the phone on his desk. Clint called Sergio, who immediately called Changuinola on another line. They waited and chatted about Bocas Town for about eight minutes when Sergio said there was an indication of some excess digitalin. The time might have reduced the reading. Clint thanked him and hung up.

"I have to find two things," Clint said slowly. "Were they here? Who else was at that tienda?"

"Tienda?"

"He stopped to have a juice at a roadside tienda, then went on up the mountain and died. There's possibly digitalin involved."

"I see."

They talked for a few more minutes, then Clint went to ask Irena if she could find if Andres and/or Filomena were out of town on the fourteenth. Maybe shopping in David.

She nodded and read through a few papers she had, then called a number. "A friend I made in town. A friend who knows a lot of things about a lot of people she ... Jelda! Ola! How are you?"

"Yes. It seems like that sometimes."

"Me? I'd tell him to walk twenty meters out on the bridge, turn right, and walk twenty more!"

"Not all of them. The good ones are rare."

"Yeah. I just wanted to see how ... oh! I just remembered! That Andres asshole. Did you say he was in David when Fanny told you about him?"

"Ain't that the truth! I suppose she stayed here to cause everyone within a kilometer grief!"

"Both of them!? A respite for the whole town!"

"Alma. Alma Vargas. She's great and knows just

how to hide the bad parts.

"Oh! Got to run! Cop shit! Hasta lluego!"

She turned to grin at Clint. "They were both supposed to be in Santiago for three or four days on the fourteenth."

"It gets more and more complicated. Thanks. I'll have to go to the mountains. I have to see what this is about.

"Maybe Santiago, first. It's on the way."

"Keep in touch, okay? I'm more than a little interested in this one!"

Clint called the station and asked that the chopper be ready to take him back toward Bocas. He grabbed a bite and went to the chopper. The pilot said, "Bocas Town or Changuinola?"

"Santiago. I don't want them to know where I'm going."

They chatted a bit. The pilot, Jorge, said he shouldn't say anything, but he knew a cop on rotation he served with in Puerto Armuelles, once. Some of this bunch were crooked as corkscrews, but he didn't say anything.

Clint nodded. He said he figured that in two minutes of getting there. Only one little group of them, but they were there and they were corrupt.

They landed in Santiago. Clint said he may be there ten minutes or a couple hours, so stay fairly close. He went to several hotels. He found that

Andres and Filomena had stayed at the Grand for one night, then had gone to David. Clint went to the chopper and said, "David. I wish Tonio was still there!"

He had to stay overnight in David, but covered the whole place. They hadn't stayed there.

He got another idea and called Silvio at the comarca not far from Rambala. He would have an answer in an hour or so.

"We might as well go on to ... Chiriqui Grande. I have an idea! That would be where they stayed, in all likelihood!'

Four hours later he knew they hadn't stayed in Chiriqui Grande. Silvio called to say some people in Punta Peña said they sounded like two people who were there for a couple of days. They were staying with Addy Gomez. They were gone in about three days.

He wanted to know who Addy Gomez was, but it would wait.

He took the bus to the tienda where Henry had stopped for a juice. There were three people there, locals, who he chatted with for about three quarters of an hour. A number of people came in cars, stopped for a juice or to use the portable restroom behind, then went on. He went to talk with the woman who ran the place when they were the only two there for a few minutes. He asked if she remembered Henry.

"Oh, yes. He came here before he died. He didn't look very good and went to the restroom twice while he was here. He rested for only a few minutes and then went on. I was a little worried, but he didn't seem too bad."

"I see. I talked with his doctor. He had heart problems. You couldn't know.

"Did any others stop while he was here?"

"Yes. People stop all the time. There were some gringos and a few Panameños. The school was out and there were some students, but they left soon because classes would start at two. I can't remember anyone special."

"Did he leave the juice on the counter when he went to the baños?"

"Oh, I think so. Everyone does."

"People came and went while he was in the baños?"

"Probably. There were a lot stopping at that time of day. He stayed in there for a long time once. I think maybe he wasn't feeling well.

"I remember! He went in when the bus came and stayed until it was leaving! A man said he would piss behind it because he couldn't make the bus wait forever! I sold six or seven juices!"

"I see. Well, no one could have seen he wasn't feeling well if he was in there while they were here."

"No. It was sad."

Clint went back to Chiriqui Grande and told the pilot he wouldn't need the chopper anymore. He would take the bus to Almirante when he finished what he was doing. The chopper left and he caught the local bus for Mali. He got out in Punta Peña and asked where Addy Gomez lived. Jaime, a friend who lived there, said it was just down the second side road, but she wasn't there. She had been gone for more than two months. His wife watched the place and reported anything to the aunt and uncle who came every once in awhile. They had only come once since she left this time. She went to Texas for several months each year.

Damnit all! Everything he found had several answers!

He headed back to Almirante. He wanted to spend tonight at home with his wife and kid.

"Okay. I have a lot of things to add up. They add up in different ways. Everything fits three different solutions. I have to have that one more thing to see which it was."

"I'm of the opinion he was murdered," Sergio replied. "What? Three different scenarios as to who killed him?"

"It was one of two people – or both – if that's what happened. It adds up too well for any of the possibilities. This might be one where someone gets away with something. It gets rid of a corrupt little clique in the police department in Chitre, so is positive for that part. It might also get rid of a couple or three people who were described as thoroughly despicable. I've never met them, but the records and people's opinions make it likely they're the scum of the earth type.

"I have a problem with the records as you got them from Chitre about Henry. Too many people there had a much higher opinion of him than the record indicates. He was definitely not disliked by his close neighbors. His doctor was entirely in sympathy with him .I think a lot of that negative information was put on his records because he was fighting the corruption. They're the ones who write up those records. The cop who was questioning things in the system there was transferred out. I think there should be a recom-mendation for him to take over when Irena tags those crooks in the police. Ninety percent of them are doing a damned good job, ten percent are the problem."

"Yes. That's the way it is about everywhere. It remains to be seen if they'll be made examples of.

"Enough of this. Let's see what we have and where we can go with it."

"I'm afraid we can't be too sure of anything, but that might not matter. I doubt there's anyone in that end of it who doesn't deserve worse!"

"What's your favorite theory?"

"I don't have a favorite. I just want to get to the truth for my personal satisfaction. I want Henry Knotts to be what I hope he was. I have to know one or two other things, then I want ... I have to call Doug. He might give me something I can work with."

Sergio shrugged. He didn't have a clue as to what Clint was talking about. Clint called Doug, a computer expert.

"Doug, I have a Trojan virus in a computer vault. I think I know the trigger, but I'm not sure. I don't have any way to know if I'll get the result I want if I open it.

"Mainly, I have to know where it came from."

"Go to the information list and look at source. It will tell you which e-mail or download carried it, which isn't really the source."

"It has a question mark at the source."

"Then it was developed on that computer. Why is it in the vault?"

"That answers part of it. Is there any way to tell what it will do if I open it?"

"Not really. Is it an exe file?"

"Yes."

"It inserts a program. What that program does isn't readable, except in basic. To put it in basic means you open it."

"Can I copy it and take it out of the vault and open it on another computer?"

"I don't think I'd take the chance, personally. I'd delete it."

"Can I take a secret file off of that computer and save it?"

"As a unit, probably not. You can copy Disk C and run the whole thing onto another computer. Make it an old clunker so you don't care if you lose everything, including the hard drive."

They talked a bit more, then Clint sighed and said he had to go back to Chitre, then shook his head and called Irena.

"Anybody go into the house?"

"No, but they're sniffing around a lot. They're wondering if it's watched."

"Can you get in and send me a copy of Disk C from the computer?"

"If you tell me how."

"Put in a four gig or better memory stick ... that's a forty gig drive, but there was only three point eight used. Open it to the Disk C icon on My Computer and right click, then click 'send' to copy it onto the memory stick. It might be a good idea to take the hard drive out of that computer and store it somewhere safe."

"I'll give it a go. How do I take the hard drive out?"

"It's the black plastic box under the power transformer, which is a metal box on top with the fan blowing out the back. It's held into place with a screw in the side. Slip it out and it's got a connector plug along the back. Unplug it and you have the hard drive."

"I can do that. I have a book to look it up in if I run into problems."

"Clint?" Sergio said. He was standing there, listening.

"Yo?"

"Does that computer have an internet modem? Is it online?"

"Yes."

"Do the same thing, but have it sent to the code for here instead of to a memory stick. We can put it directly on the stick here and save a couple of days getting that one here."

It was on speaker. Irena said she would do that. Sergio gave her the contact code, so she could directly upload to the police computer. She would call as soon as she was in the place and had the computer online. She was going to add a small thing.

They waited. It was forty minutes later when she called and said it was ready. Sergio clicked the "accept" when the request came for access. The drive ran on download for more than six minutes, then shut down. Clint called Irena and said it was received. She said she had the side of the computer open and would take out the hard drive. She had brought one with her from a shop the main office told her about that she would plug in. It was gibberish, so maybe whoever would think the virus had worked.

Clint thanked her and said it might be time to open a virus vault and see what monster popped out.

Monster Mash

Clint inserted the memory stick into an old HP computer USB port the police had in a closet. It was one that had been replaced and kept there for emergencies that never happened. The others were erased completely with a government wipe program and donated to the primary schools, which require a lot of computer use knowledge before graduation. It was decided some years ago that the modern world required a basic knowledge of computers.

The copy of the hard drive disk would carry the entire virus program, as well as what was in the vault. He went to the program and clicked on the virus program and moved it back into "programs" on the hard drive.

He then went to the secret file and opened it. The screen flickered a few times. Nothing else seemed to happen.

He carefully studied the screen and saw a new secondary window listed on the work bar below. He clicked on it.

The screen cleared and Notepad came on. The hourglass stayed on for a few seconds, then the message was there on the screen.

Mr. Faraday:

I can only hope it is you who are reading this. I am quite sure the excuse for police technicians we have in this station will have either deleted this program or opened it inside the vault, which would accomplish the same thing.

I will give you some background, then explain what I have done and why.

I am Henry Joseph Knotts, son of a North American man, Joseph Ringling Knotts, from Topeka, Kansas, USA. I was born, 1973, to a Colombian/Panamanian woman, Dolores Sylva C. Dolores was a dual citizen when she became an executive for a German company in the Canal Zone. I was born there. My father and mother were married formally in Panamá. I am, therefore, a true Panamanian (and proud to be!). I received my education in Panamá until I reached the age of seventeen, when I was sent to Kansas for my university education. I was, of course, also a citizen of the USA because my father was and I was born in the Canal Zone.

I was most surprised and delighted to find that I was far ahead of most gringo (I must think of them as that) students my own age. The schools in

Panamá are very good.

Be that as it may, I earned a BS in physics and returned to Panamá to work with an engineer who designs special equipment used in many things. I met Filomena Sardina and married her in 2004.

My life had been quite pleasant, comparatively speaking, until that time. I was working at a job that paid, for here, exceptionally well.

I learned very soon that my lovely wife was not the person she had pretended to be. She was a schemer who tricked a gringo into marriage to make an easy life for herself. The situation was turning rapidly sour.

I had, for some time, felt a pressure inside my skull. That is the only way I can describe it. It was not actually painful, but it wasn't exactly unpainful, either. I was diagnosed with a small inoperable cancer just above the medula.

I was under a great deal of stress with my wife. I had some heart pain and a mild attack. I was diagnosed with mild stress-related heart muscle deterioration that was accelerating. I must find a less stressful living situation.

I quit my job. I had plenty of money saved and my wife's brother, Andres Vanderas, was living in Chitre, where he worked for a large Colombian company.

I came to Chitre and found the area much to my

liking. I bought a small property and built a comfortable house. I found a doctor, Rosendo Rodriguez, who was much better than the team of doctors I was consulting in the Canal Zone.

I did not care for Andres. He is a shady type of person who is dealing with some very suspicious people. He had influence with the police and courts through what was obviously bribery. He and Filomena had relatives in the police.

Filomena and I soon had strong disagreements and I was thinking of divorce. I had once caught her in a situation that was basic infidelity. She always denied any such outside relationships. She announced she was pregnant in February of 2006. Our son, José, was born in October.

We stayed together for the child, or so I thought, for some time. We were arguing more and more and she one night attacked me with a knife when I charged her with infidelity. She had just come home from an assignation. I forced her from the house as a bad influence on our son. She claimed that I didn't know if he was really my son or not, but she did.

Several times I had called the police when she was drinking and acting violently. They refused to respond for a reason I didn't connect, at the time. It later became evident it was because her cousin, Carla Dorcas, was the police dispatcher. The two times when there remained a transcript of my domestic complaint showed that she never dispatched the patrol to my domicile.

Filomena and Andres' relatives and friends permeate throughout the entire judicial system here. There aren't actually very many, but they are in positions to guarantee those two, and a few others, are never charged or prosecuted for anything in Chitre.

My health was deteriorating. I had to remove myself from the conditions in my personal life or would soon die, leaving my son with no real protection against those people. I could somewhat ameliorate the situation for him by my presence as a threat to Filomena and Andres and their corrupt family.

I knew it was hopeless for me to in any way affect them in Chitre because their powerful family members in the courts would guarantee they would not be charged, much less prosecuted, for the many things they were doing.

The situation became worse and worse. My health was deteriorating more rapidly. I filed for divorce in Panamá City, where she had no undue influence on the court or its decision. I charged her with repeated infidelity and was able to have four persons testify to personal and positive knowledge that such was the case.

The divorce was to be granted. I then demanded custody of my son. She claimed he was not my son. I demanded DNA codification of the truth or untruth of that statement, but demanded custody, in either case, as she was not a fit parent.

She refused the DNA codification, but my son and I were tested and it was found that there was but one chance in eight billion that he was not my son. She then claimed that my health situation was such that I could not guarantee the boy a secure and continuing situation.

Mr. Faraday, she has demonstrated many times that she was not truly concerned for the boy. She was trying to keep some control on my life.

I have an aunt, Marta Bellinger, in a town called Mariato in Veraguas. I passed custody to her to establish a stable life for the child. She loves José deeply and was most pleased that I think so highly of her. She is unable to bear children and was taking care of several local children in bad family situations.

Filomena has not one time used her visitation rights, which shows the truth of my statements about her.

I have become very bitter, not because of my health or such matters. That is part of life over which we have little control. I am bitter because I was so badly used by these horrible examples of human refuse. They prey on people and use them to their own profit. They are vultures. They are the worst kinds of snakes.

I have, for the past year, been most carefully documenting the things Filomena, Andres, a judge, D. V. Melendez V. Carla Dorcas. Fernando Flako V. José (my son was not named for that slimy snake!) Perez C. et al. I have placed that information and documentation and proof in photographs and audio disks in a large carton that is among the items in the bodega at my house. The carton has household papers on the top, with the pertinent parts below. It is labeled Rcpts.2004-2010 and is between Rcpts. 1998-2003 and Rcpts. 2010-, which is in front and is where I toss receipts. I arrange and list them each January. They would never think of looking for anything there. Filomena often chided me for keeping old records. She throws everything away after two years. Most, she throws away when she receives them.

Clint stopped and grabbed the phone to call Irena. "Go to the house! The bodega! A carton labeled R-C-P-T-S two thousand four through two thousand ten! It has all the evidence you could ask for, documented!"

"Really?!"

"Filomena, Melendez, Flako, Dorcas, Perez,

Andres. Very carefully recorded with proof.”

“I could kiss you!”

“You need a reason like that?”

“Not really. You’re just too married.”

“Picture a fist with the middle finger extended.”

She laughed. Clint explained he was in the middle, so might call again. He went back to the screen.

... away when she receives them. She is, as a result, always trying to remember when she bought something or how much she paid for it or various other things it can be simple to resolve by finding a receipt or copy of a check

You will find, in that carton, information that is unproven about a number of others. Perhaps an investigation can use the information included to put an end to several corrupt groups.

My health is deteriorating badly now. I have not finished what I planned and know well that I never will. I can, however, attempt to have someone else continue with the process. My only problem at this point is to ensure that the process will continue. If it must go through this group, it is halted before it is begun.

I came across your name several times in the newspapers and on the television when you thwarted just such plans and schemes among some very powerful and dangerous people. I am thus sending this to your e-mail address. The computer program will send it the moment the computer is turned on after being unused for seven days. I will be dead, but what I have learned will be transmitted to a person who I feel is caring about such things.

Please, Mr. Faraday! **<u>Stop</u>** *these crooks!*

Henry Joseph Knotts, deceased.

Clint sat back. He mumbled, "You got your wish, Henry. Thanks for being what I'd hoped you were!"

He saved the message to the memory stick and was about to get up when the computer dinged. He looked at the screen and saw a digital clock moving backward in seconds. There were eleven seconds left. It reached zero and a page came on the screen:

Mr. Faraday

This is added six days after the above and is for your eyes only, please. Others would find cause to interfere with what must happen as I now see it.

I have come to this decision because I want to be totally honest with you and because a usable situation has arisen.

Filomena has an aunt who lives in Punta Peña for nine months of the year and in the USA three months of the year. She is now in the USA. Filomena and her brother will go to Punta Peña for a few days to check on the property there. She does this every year. Punta Peña is in Bocas del Toro. You are in Bocas del Toro. I can be sure you will receive the necessary facts by what I am going to do.

That bunch can stop almost anything in Chitre. They have garnered the power through corrupt practices and may now use blackmail to ensure their schemes are carried out. I feel it is far too possible they would stop investigation if there is not a way to stop them.

I believe you will understand that my plan can be thwarted if it is shown that it is a setup.

Investigation of most crimes can be halted or subverted through use of the persons and offices being blackmailed. Those people are caught in a steel trap of their own design. They have to live in fear that they will be exposed. They are drawn ever deeper into the sordidity of the affair.

I thus have added this to show to you that I am being as honest as I know how to be with you. I realize that the cancer can make a viewpoint that is logical and sure to the one in that perspective unintelligible to others. Dr. Rodriguez assures me this is not the case with me, but I must be sure that I am not as bad as those I would expose.

If what has come before is such to you, please act according to your conscience concerning it. I have tried to be exact and thorough.

If what has come before is logical and provable, continue with this.

Here is my thought process and reasoning:

Clint sat back to consider. Henry had made a concise and provable case, so far. It was clear that he was a very careful person who wouldn't try to stretch truths or invent theories to present as fact. This was definitely complete enough that Irena would put a fast end to the bunch in Chitre. A number of them were going to spend a lot of time in jail. Henry had guaranteed that by what had happened. Why was this part ... of course! Any number of things would mean the information never got past the Chitre police department if it was there. It had to be brought to the attention of someone who could have it moved from Chitre to Panamá City. The influence could extend as far as Santiago, but not to the main offices.

Henry had accomplished that by dying with that note in Bocas del Toro. Clint was known and respected by the police department there. Full attention would be paid to the note.

Clint sighed and scrolled down to the next part of the message:

... my reasoning: many crimes can be hidden when they are not of importance to get higher

levels of investigation involved. My merely dying would not get that attention. It would all be for nothing, in the long run.

My situation, as described, put me in constant danger of being killed to ensure my silence. I too obviously knew too much. There were actual threats that were never acted upon here in Chitre when they were immediately halted at the point of the complaint being taken.

There is one complaint report that was not erased included in the above cache. Andres and Filomena stated quite flatly that I wouldn't live to see the light of tomorrow if I ever made another complaint against them. I then entered that threat complaint and it was saved, meaning they dared not act against me, at least for a time. Murder will be investigated. If there are no results locally, Panamá City will send a special crew, especially if it is a gringo or higher profile case. They must save the complaint for defense, should anyone, including the person who filed the complaint, question Panamá City about resolution. I doubt not that the complaint has disappeared from the records in Chitre, since I died in another place. You will have that copy at hand to present and to question why it no longer remains in the records, greatly strengthening evidence against them as being my murderers.

Yes, Mr. Faraday, I intend to make this look as though I was murdered by those people to shut me up about what I have found.

This will be what happens. Please do not reveal this until your day in court, if you must do so. I am in hope you will see what I have done and will agree with my goals. There are times, rarely, I admit, when the end justifies the means. You are intelligent and will know this.

(1) I am dying. I am in constant discomfort that is fast approaching pain. I have an inoperable cancer that can – and would – kill me at any time. I also have a heart condition that is fast approaching a fatal stage, without great care.

I have dedicated the past few years of my life to stopping some of the human vultures who prey on innocent people through corruption and criminal acts.

(2) I have complaints about threats to my life made by these very same vultures.

(3) I must find a way to expose these people.

(4) I cannot hope that exposure will come forth if the entire process is left here in Chitre. Even Santiago, where there is some chance I could bring it to the attention of the proper people, is most unsure.

(5) I have read and heard much of a person, Clint Faraday, in Bocas del Toro, who pursues

such matters with a vengeance and who is not corruptible. This person would be a certain way to accomplish the removal of these people. If I can get his attention, my hopes of success in the final chapter of my life are greatly enhanced.

(6) Two of the persons on record as threatening my life will be in Bocas del Toro in a few days. Due to the fact the records and proofs I am leaving show conspiracy in criminal acts among the group, Faraday can bring resolution of most of it.

(7) Murder is always investigated thoroughly.

(8) It will be easy to make my death appear to be the result of murder. If I am found dead in a place and situation that would tend to indicate a possibility of murder, it would be investigated as murder. AND if that investigation were to be conducted by Clinton Faraday its solution is assured.

(9) A natural death, where there is also strong probability of, shall we say, an assist, such as dying of a heart condition where there is digitalin found in the body, will guarantee it is murder.

(10) There is a place in Bocas del Toro where one may walk for two kilometers, always upward, to find a spectacular view of the Caribbean Sea and the islands of Bocas del Toro archipelago. Such a walk would stress a heart. There is a small

tienda that sells juices and snacks at that place. Many people stop on that road at the tienda for refreshment and to use the facilities there. It can be depended on that some of those who stop will be strangers to the area. It is a spot where one may leave a juice on the counter when he uses the facilities. If a person were to be in the restroom while several other persons were at the counter, if that person were later found dead at the viewpoint of a heart attack, if the heart attack were to be shown to have been assisted by a dose of digitalin, murder would be as much as proven. The only ones in the area who may be involved are two who there is a complaint of threat on the life of the dead person were in the near area, if the digitalin could only have been applied while a juice was on a counter, while the victim was in the restroom, those two would have no defense and would be convicted of the crime.

Mr. Faraday, I leave this in fear that I may be affected in my mind by the cancer and may be wrong about these people from personal enmity. Should that prove the case, I know you are an honest man who would expose what I have done. If your investigation, which will be thorough, shows that was not the case, I know you will have the practicality to know there is no other way to fight such people at this time and in this place.

If, indeed, we are possessed of an immortal spirit I sincerely hope to meet you in person somewhen.

Your very true friend, though I have never met you, Henry –

Clint sat back to think. This was one hell of a load to put on a person.

Hell! He had broad shoulders!

He turned off the computer and slipped the memory stick into his pocket. "I'm going home to be with the wife and son for awhile. I guess I'll have to appear in court on this one."

"Well, probably they won't plead. They don't have a chance! This is as solid a case as we ever get!" Sergio replied.

Should Clint tell Sergio about the second part of that message?

Sergio didn't need that on him. He had enough.

"It damned well looks that way! Caio!"

He went to his wife and son. This was now a matter of waiting. Irena would have a very solid case for a lot of things. She would get definite convictions for the whole bunch. Clint wasn't needed for that.

The problem for him was that the sentences would be minimal for the corruption unless a conspiracy to commit murder were a part of it.

He thought about it. They were, as described, despicable.

He got a call from Irena. Court. Panamá City. Four days. He was needed.

"I'll be there."

"... because of his medication, he saw things that weren't there. He took some ambiguous photographs and made up something to fit. He made complaints against his wife and her brother, including the other of my clients and added them to misunderstood times and situations and came up with an answer that had nothing to do with the equation, the facts.

"In short, this is, while possibly not intentional, a total fabrication!

"Thank you, your honor."

Defense attorney Geraldo Rincón sat. The judge wrote on her pad, then looked at Irena.

"Your honor, this was a thorough investigation that began as the investigation of a murder, as explained in the initial declaration. The rest of it simply happened as a result of that investigation.

"What we ask the court to consider in light of that is that, had there been no murder, this would not be before you at this time. It is before you because the murder, not the other criminal acts, are what this trial is about.

"A murder, to be proven, must usually have a

shown motive. This murder has no motive, except for the material presented.

"The murder was by conspiracy and becomes basic to all other charges. The criminal charges could be argued, as the learned counsel stated, as merely fabrications of a mind being influenced by medication, as the doctor has assured us was not the case.

"Let's allow Mr. Clinton Faraday, the primary investigator in the case, to present what he found. You know Mr. Faraday's reputation for never accepting a story until it is certainly proven. His record is exemplary!"

"I'll hear Mr. Faraday for the record and so that the defense may question him on any pertinent points," the judge said. Irena almost exclaimed at the "... for the record" part while the defense deflated. The evidence certainly didn't support the defense in any way. "Mr. Faraday, briefly, if you will?"

"Thank you, Your Honor.

"This is a definite case. There are only two ways it could have happened, both of which have shown to be with the defense guilty. Only the conspiracy part is in question.

"Consider: a man with a mild heart condition and a small cancer in remission is investigating official corruption in an important town. He has compiled very definite and positive evidence and has recorded it most carefully. The persons under suspicion are aware he has that evidence.

"This man knows he will eventually die from that cancer. It is inoperable and in remission, not cured. Someday it will emerge from that remission and will kill him. That is a fact he knows there's no hiding from. He has accepted it.

"That man also loved Panamá. He wanted to see everything he could before he died. He wasn't interested in cities. They are all, basically, alike. They held no appeal. He wanted to see the real Panamá and photograph it from the best places.

"He is aware his evidence will be erased by the very ones it is held against, under normal circumstances, so he makes a complete record of all of it and always carries a message to a person he knows is as tenacious as he when it comes to those acts that hurt what we call 'The average Joe' in a place. If anything untoward happens to him, that message will be delivered.

"He goes to view a special place, to take some special photographs. It entails, because of his desire to fully experience the area, walking for two kilometers along a constant rise. It will stress his heart, somewhat, but he knows it isn't critical, that all he has to do is rest for a few minutes if he gets symptoms of overstress.

"He stops at a small tienda, where everyone seems to stop for refreshment to rest and to use the facilities before proceeding. He is a little stressed, but the short stop will allow that stress, physical stress, to subside. He is in no danger from it.

"He leaves his juice on a counter while he uses the facilities. That is the general practice. There are a number of people around, including many from a bus that had stopped for the refreshments. Most buses will stop if the clients request it.

"He drinks the juice, bids farewell to the people there and proceeds on up the mountain.

"He is later found dead near the spot he wished to photograph.

"Now for the *meanwhile* aspects of the case, as I see it.

"A man is a direct and immediate threat to a group who have already made threats against his life. He has accumulated a lot of proof of their misdeeds. His proofs will send them to jail for what they have done.

"That man, who has a slightly weak heart, goes to a spot to take photographs that requires he climb, if not greatly, for two kilometers. He stops for a juice at that spot, two kilometers away.

"He has his juice. He uses the restroom when it was half finished, leaving it on the counter while he used the facilities. A number of people are around the juice stand.

"The man proceeds to near the spot he wishes to photograph. He dies there.

"A very important factor here is that his body had digitalin, a heart medicine he *did not use* in it. The doctor has stated that was the immediate probable cause of death.

"Because of the timing, we know the digitalin was administered while he was at that juice stand where he used the facilities and left the juice standing on the counter.

"He died. He did not use digitalin.

"There were two, and only two, people he had ever known or been involved with. Those two were also two who were in the conspiracy and corruption proofs. Those two were the only ones in that area at that time who had any reason whatever to want him silenced.

"Your honor, the way that adds up is pretty much the way two and two add up. There is only one answer we can accept: Directly or indirectly, this group represents the reason behind the death, declared by the police to be murder, of Henry Joseph Knotts.

"Knotts' life was made unpleasant enough by these people for the past few years. His death was the ultimate act that can be allowed to be caused by these people.

"I humbly ask that the court deliver justice to Henry Joseph Knotts and his child! The justice will automatically extend to his ex-wife and the others involved. That's what justice is.

"Thank you, Your Honor."

"Thank you, Mr. Faraday. Your testimony is brief and damning. It reinforces the court's case for conviction nicely. It adds up as it must. Two and two has but one answer."

"Answers we can accept, Your Honor. I have no doubt mathematicians can come up with other answers, the same as lawyers can always come up with other answers. It is simply a matter of acceptable answers."

"Very astute, Mr. Faraday. A lawyer will say that two and two equal four, but only when you *interpret* it that way.

"Does defense counsel have any questions of this witness?"

"I most certainly do!" Lcda. Villamos declared hotly. "I want to know how Mr. Faraday can sit there and say my clients were at some tienda at some certain time! Can he show proof of that? They were *not there*!"

"I didn't," Clint replied.

"Er? You sat right there and said that my clients put digitalin in his drink at that juice stand, that it was the only time it could have been administered!"

"I said no such thing."

"You honor! You heard him!"

"I did not hear any such statement. Recorder?"

She looked through her tape. "There was no such statement made."

"What was stated? I was certain he said...." Villamos asked.

"There were people ... a bus ... that because of the timing, was the only place it could have ... no mention of your clients."

"Thank you, recorder. Anything else?"

"But he *did* mention my clients! It was about that tienda and the digitalin!"

"Recorder?"

She went through the tape and said, *He died. He did not use digitalin. There were two, and only two, people he had ever known or been involved with. Those two were also two who were in the conspiracy and corruption proofs. Those two were the only ones in that area at that time who had any reason whatever to want him silenced.*

"There was no mention that those two people were ever at the tienda."

"And then he said that about two and two," the judge said. "Anything else?"

Villamos looked confused and went toward her

seat, then turned back, "Mr. Faraday, did you, or did you not, state that my clients were the only ones there who could have been at that tienda to administer that digitalin to a glass of juice?"

"I did not. I only stated that they were the only ones in the area who had motive. Whether or not they personally put digitalin in a glass at that tienda at that times is, admittedly, unstated. I merely pointed out that they were the only ones in the area, *that we know of*, who had motive. If there was anyone else, please so inform. I will investigate to see what they were doing there. As this is conspiracy, that person or those persons cannot be among the persons the evidence was against. It doesn't matter one whit which of the people in a conspiracy actually commit the crime, only that it was one or more of them."

"Nothing further," Villamos announced and sat, glaring at her clients sitting around the table. Clint supposed it had dawned on her that the specific person didn't matter. It only had to be anyone of them. Her case was lost!

"Court in recess," the judge called. She went out the door behind her seat. No one doubted her return would be for sentencing. It was a non-jury type of trial by request of the defense. With what and how this case was presented a jury would probably demand the death sentence they didn't have in Panamá for that type of thing. With this judge, they would all serve seven to ten years.

It was ten.

"Well! It all came out pretty good at the trial, didn't it?" Sergio asked. "If there was ever a solid case for murder, this was it!

"It was on television when the judge came out and said the sentence was ten years for all of them. That Dorcas woman screaming and the Andres character swearing he would get them all for that!"

"The best part was when the judge said making threats in court was contempt. She added two years to his sentence. Great show!" Judi said.

"Oh, Clint always has a case sewed up tight and right down to what really happened before he presents it to the court," Tyna said.

"Not always," Clint replied.

C. D. Moulton's works are available on most major outlets as printed or e-books. CD writes the CD Grimes, PI, mysteries, the Det. Lt. Nick Storie mysteries, the Clint Faraday mysteries, the Flight of the Maita science fiction series, books on orchid culture and many others of many types. Mystery, adventure, intrigue, science fiction, humor, fantasy, paranormal, mild erotica, and factual.